# Princess
# of the Full Moon

By FREDERIC GUIRMA / Translated by John Garrett

THE MACMILLAN COMPANY / Collier-Macmillan Ltd., London

End paper masks one, two and three are worn during the ceremony in which
aspirants are initiated into the secret society of the Gurunsi and Senoufo
tribes. Mask one is Gurunsi and represents a genie; mask two is Senoufo and
represents a wild boar; mask three is known as a Bobo, or monkey mask.
Mask four is a funeral mask of the Mossi tribe and represents an antelope.

To the children of David Chastagner,
who was born in the village of Koubri
some forty years ago

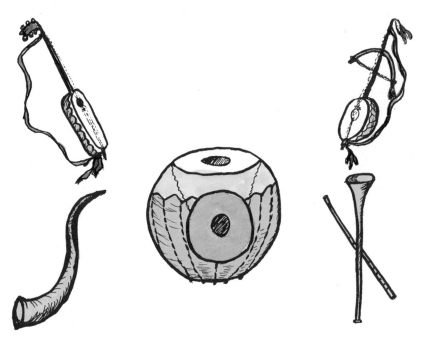

## PRONUNCIATION

Kiugu Peulgo = cúe goo   peârl gō
Pind'n' Bang Boumbu = pĭnd'n'  báng  bóom boo
Wintosuka = wín toe sōo k̆a
Yung'suka = yúng' sōo k̆a

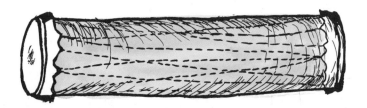

Long ago in the heart of Africa there lived a king who had a beautiful daughter. She was called Kiugu Peulgo, which means "Full Moon." She was tall and slender, with long fine hands and a lovely face, and her skin was smooth and black as ebony. When the time came for her to marry, handsome princes, brave nobles and mighty warriors arrived at the capital to court her. They came from far and wide, dressed in their richest robes and finest armor, accompanied by their servants and retainers.

Princess Kiugu Peulgo was well aware that she was the prettiest girl in the land, and so much tribute to her beauty had turned her head. She decided that loveliness such as hers deserved a husband of equal perfection. The man she married must have no flaw, no scar of any kind. The princess turned down one suitor after another. One had fought a dragon and his shoulder still bore the print of its claw; another was marked by a battle wound; a third, by a spear cut received during a war game; and so it went. Soon the line of departing suitors and their followers, all mounted on horses and camels, raised clouds of dust that covered the horizon. The king wanted to see his daughter married and was growing more and more impatient.

The young shepherd who took care of Kiugu Peulgo's sheep was secretly in love with the princess. He was hunchbacked and ugly, and his body was covered with scars from wounds he had received while fighting the wild animals that attacked his flock. All he had was a flute and a parakeet to keep him company.

Each morning and night he would seat himself beneath
the princess's window and play the same melancholy song
about a beautiful girl who had been kidnaped by a monster.
Sometimes he would set aside his flute and sing the words:

> Wood chopper, wood chopper,
> go tell my mother.
> Wood chopper, wood chopper,
> go tell my father.
> Everyone lives at home,
> but I live with death.

One morning, not long after the last of the suitors had departed, the sound of trumpets was heard in the distance. Soon it became known that the heir to the kingdom of Pind'n' Bang Boumbu was on his way to seek the hand of Kiugu Peulgo.

Even before he arrived word came that he was attended by a retinue of dazzling splendor. He was preceded by one hundred musicians riding a hundred camels with saddles decorated in gold and silver. The musicians were followed by one hundred more camels bearing gifts of gold and precious jewels for the princess. The prince himself and his warriors mounted on one hundred horses made up the rear. Princess Kiugu Peulgo watched the prince's arrival from the roof of the palace. She thought he was the handsomest man she had ever seen. Perhaps at last she had found her husband.

The king's physicians examined the young prince and there was not a blemish on his body. At last the great bull horn trumpets blared out the news that Kiugu Peulgo, Princess of the Full Moon, was to be married to the Prince of Pind'n' Bang Boumbu.

The wedding celebration lasted for seven days and seven nights. No one could recall such beautiful ladies and handsome warriors in all their finery, such feasting and games. Only the poor shepherd was sad. He sat among his lambs on a hill overlooking the city, his flute at his side and his parakeet on his shoulder.

When the wedding was over the prince prepared to take his princess back to Pind'n' Bang Boumbu. The shepherd came down from the hill to say farewell. He begged the princess to honor him by accepting his flute as a wedding gift, but she only laughed and refused to take it. As the shepherd turned away he caught the eye of the Prince of Pind'n' Bang Boumbu and was filled with foreboding. Again he implored the princess to accept his gift.

"Your royal highness," pleaded the shepherd, "should you ever be in danger you need only to play the wood chopper song on this flute and help will come."

The proud princess grew furious. "Who are you, ugly shepherd," she cried, "to dare tell Kiugu Peulgo what to do?"

Seeing the princess's anger, her husband asked:

"Who is this worm who dares approach you?"

"He is my shepherd," the princess replied.

"Your shepherd?" shouted the prince. "I will have him killed for his insolence!"

Angry as she was the princess did not want her shepherd killed. She begged her husband to spare his life and at last he agreed.

Before the caravan left the shepherd managed to hide his flute in a pack on the princess's horse.

The journey to Pind'n' Bang Boumbu was a long one. For the first ten days the prince and all his entourage did everything to entertain the princess: musicians played, singers sang, the warriors ran races up and down the hills.

But on the tenth day, the prince suddenly stopped speaking to his wife. On the eleventh day, the hundred musicians, mounted on a hundred camels, vanished into thin air. On the twelfth day, the hundred camels, loaded with treasure, disappeared from sight. On the thirteenth day, the hundred nobles and warriors, riding a hundred horses, were no longer to be seen. The prince and princess remained alone.

"Where are your men?" asked the princess.

"They have gone to where they came from. You must ask no questions," the prince replied, and they rode on toward Pind'n' Bang Boumbu.

On the fourteenth day, they stopped in the middle of a lonely forest. The prince dismounted and said, "I will be right back. Wait for me here." When he had disappeared from sight he gave the splendor of his robes back to the wild flowers that grew there. His diamonds he returned to the dew and their sparkle to the rays of the sun. When he came back to the princess she cried out:

"My prince, where are your royal robes?"

"They have been returned to their proper owners. You must ask no questions," the prince replied.

When they had gone some distance farther they stopped
once more and the prince said:

"I will be right back. Wait for me here." When he had
disappeared from sight he gave back to the doe the softness
of his eyes; to the giraffe, the grace of his movements; to the
lion, the majesty of his pause; to the snake, the smoothness
of his skin.

And now a monster returned to the princess. His body was covered with hair, his eyes were like burning coals, his teeth were huge and sharp. He pulled the princess from her horse by her hair, threw her over his shoulder, and roaring like a lion carried her to a cave in the depth of a desolate mountain. There he thrust her into the darkest corner and said:

"Spoiled, stupid daughter of a stupid king! You wanted a perfect husband and see what you have now! In fourteen days I will roast you over my fire and feed you to my giant fish that live in a lake under this mountain. Until then repent for your vanity and foolishness." The monster left the cave and hurried away.

The princess began to weep. She wept so much and so long that her tears formed a pool that trickled out of the cave and down the mountainside. She thought of all the noble princes she had turned away, and even of the poor, ugly shepherd. "I would have been better off married to him than to this monster," she said to herself. At last she dried her tears and decided that since she was to die she would die bravely as a princess should. She opened her pack to choose her most beautiful gown and as she pulled it forth the flute the shepherd had hidden away fell to the ground.

Kiugu Peulgo remembered what the shepherd had told her. She quickly climbed out of the cave and up the mountain as high as she could go. There she sat down on a rock and began to play the shepherd's song. She played it again and again and when she got tired of playing she sang:

Wood chopper, wood chopper,
go tell my mother.
Wood chopper, wood chopper,
go tell my father.
Everyone lives at home,
but I live with death.

One day as the shepherd lay in the sun dreaming of the princess he felt his parakeet beat its wings wildly in his face. He leaped to his feet and far away he heard the sound of a flute playing a familiar melody.

The shepherd hurried to the palace. He broke into the throne room and told the king that his daughter was in grave danger. But the king and his courtiers only laughed: "You must be mad, you ugly fool!" said the king. "The princess has married the richest and handsomest man in the world, the Prince of Pind'n' Bang Boumbu. Go back to your sheep before I have your head cut off."

"Then I must rescue her myself," the shepherd said. "Although I do not know where to find this kingdom of Pind'n' Bang Boumbu." And he ran out of the palace.

The courtiers went on laughing at the madness of the poor shepherd, but the king became suddenly silent. "The shepherd is right," he said at last. "Where is the kingdom of Pind'n' Bang Boumbu?"

It was the oldest of the king's ministers who spoke first: "Come to think of it, in all my years I have never heard of this kingdom," and now the other ministers nodded in agreement. "Then," said the king, "we must set out at once to find the kingdom of Pind'n' Bang Boumbu and make sure that my daughter is well and happy."

The drums were beaten and the bull horns rang out. The horses were saddled, and the king rode forth at the head of his men to seek his daughter. For thirteen days they rode along led by the familiar melody of the magic flute. On the fourteenth day they heard the silver voice of the princess singing over and over again:

> Wood chopper, wood chopper,
> go tell my mother.
> Wood chopper, wood chopper,
> go tell my father.
> Everyone lives at home,
> but I live with death.

All at once a thunderous laugh rolled over the hills and the monster stood before them.

"If you have come to save your daughter, foolish king, you are too late. Turn back now while you still live!"

"Who are you?" the king cried out.

"You do not know me? I am the perfect Prince of Pind'n' Bang Boumbu."

The king drew his great sword and lunged at the monster who at once turned into a cloud and drifted away on the wind.

"Forward!" the king shouted to his men and they galloped on.

The monster had immediately become himself again and was quietly following behind the riders. One by one he changed each mounted warrior into a stone. When the king reached the foot of the mountain, the monster stopped him with a shout: "Look behind you, king! Where are your warriors?"

The king turned back and instead of his men saw a trail of white stones spread over the ground.

"These are your men, king. And now you will join them." The monster transformed the king himself into a large white rock. Then he returned to the cave where the princess now waited believing no one had heard her song. Quickly the monster built a great fire. When it blazed high he took hold of Kiugu Peulgo and was about to throw her into the flames.

"Stop!" rang out a voice from the entrance to the cave. "No princess will die today." It was the shepherd. He had been given an old nag to ride, and the king and his warriors had left him far behind. The monster let go of the princess and turned to face him.

"Who are you?" he asked.

"Don't you recognize me?" said the shepherd.

The monster was about to reply when the shepherd's parakeet flew in and perched on his shoulder.

"Now I know you!" the monster cried. "You are Wintosuka, Prince of the Noonday Sun."

Drawing his sword, the shepherd replied: "And I challenge you, Yung'suka, Devil Prince of Midnight. It was you who fed my sister to your evil fish and turned me into an ugly shepherd and my page into a parakeet. For seven years, seven months and seven days I have waited for this moment. I gave Kiugu Peulgo my magic flute to protect her against danger knowing that love could give it the power to bring me to her rescue."

The shepherd struck out at the monster, who at once turned himself into a raging lion. They fought for a day and a night without pause until at last the shepherd buried his sword deep in the lion's heart. The lion's blood streamed through the cave. The shepherd was about to cry out in victory when a great laugh echoed through the mountain.

The dying lion had become a giant. They struggled together
for three days and three nights until the shepherd struck
the giant a blow on the head and he fell to the ground. But
within a moment he had disappeared, and in his place a tiny

mosquito buzzed angrily around the cave. The parakeet chased the mosquito for a day and a night until it bit off one of the insect's wings. As the mosquito fell to the ground it became a snake with seven heads. And the shepherd battled the snake.

When the princess saw the snake with seven heads she began to despair. She drew out the flute and began to play her mournful song. For a moment the seven heads paused in a row to listen, and with one stroke of his sword the shepherd cut them off. As the snake died the shepherd was sprayed with its blood, and his enchantment was lifted. Wintosuka, Prince of the Noonday Sun, stood before the princess. He took a drop of the snake's blood and rubbed it on the parakeet, who immediately became a handsome page again. Princess Kiugu Peulgo wept for joy.

The page collected her tears in a calabash and went to the foot of the mountain. There he moistened the white rock and each white stone with her tears, and the king and his warriors sprang back to life.

The royal procession returned home

and the wedding took place at once.

Although the court astrologer announced that the exact day and hour of the marriage had been predicted by the stars, no one paid any attention to him. It was quite clear that only love had empowered the Prince of the Noonday Sun to vanquish the Devil Prince of Midnight and win the hand of the Princess of the Full Moon. The prince and princess had many handsome children and lived happily together for the rest of their lives.

The princess had learned that without love there is no perfection, and that even the noonday sun must give way to the night and the full moon must wane before daylight. As for the king, he ruled more wisely. Having discovered that there was no such kingdom as Pind'n' Bang Boumbu, he had also learned that the words meant, "You should have known."